A COLLECTION
OF LETTERS

by

JANE AUSTEN

First published in 1871

British Library Cataloguing-in-Publication Data
A catalogue record for this book is available
from the British Library

CONTENTS

JANE AUSTEN

Jane Austen was an English novelist whose works of romantic fiction, set among the landed gentry, earned her a place as one of the most widely read writers in English literature. Her realism, biting irony and social commentary have gained her historical importance among the reading public, scholars and critics alike.

Austen was born on 16th December 1775, and lived her entire life as part of a close-knit family located on the lower fringes of the English landed gentry. Biographical information on Jane Austen is incredibly scarce however, as only some personal and family letters remain. She was educated primarily by her father and older brothers as well as through her own reading. Jane spent most of her early years being schooled at home, until leaving for boarding school at the age of ten, alongside her elder sister Cassandra. They left one year later though (1786) as the family could not afford to send both of their daughters to school. According to Park Honan, a biographer of Austen, life in the Austen home was lived in 'an open, amused, easy intellectual atmosphere' where the ideas of those with whom the Austens might disagree politically or socially were 'considered and discussed.' After returning from school in 1786, Austen 'never again lived anywhere beyond the bounds of her immediate family environment.'

Her artistic apprenticeship lasted from her teenage years into her thirties. As Austen grew into adulthood, she continued to live at her parents' home, carrying out those activities normal for women of her age and social standing: she practised the fortepiano, assisted her sister and mother with supervising servants, and attended female relatives during childbirth and older relatives on their deathbeds. During this period, she experimented with various literary forms, including the epistolary novel (a novel written as a series of documents) which she then abandoned, and wrote and extensively revised three major novels and began a fourth. *Lady Susan,* written between 1793 and 1795 was an experiment of this kind; taking the form of a series of letters, it is described as Austen's most ambitious and sophisticated early work. Austen biographer Claire Tomalin describes the heroine of the novella as a 'sexual predator who uses her intelligence and charm to manipulate, betray, and abuse her victims, whether lovers, friends or family.'

In 1800, George Austen (Jane's father), announced his decision to retire from his post in the ministry and move the family to Bath. Jane Austen was incredibly unsettled and unhappy in Bath, and sadly her father passed away during this period. This left the family in a precarious financial position and in 1805 Jane, her sisters and her mother lived in rented quarters. They moved to 'Chawton Cottage' in Hampshire in 1809. A gift from Austen's brother Edward, this cottage allowed the family a more settled life and in a quieter, more tranquil setting. Austen was thus able to concentrate on her writing. From 1811 until 1816, with the release of *Sense and Sensibility* (1811), *Pride and Prejudice* (1813), *Mansfield Park* (1814) and *Emma* (1815), she achieved success as a published writer.

Through her brother Henry, the publisher Thomas Egerton agreed to issue *Sense and Sensibility,* and the earnings from the novel provided Austen with some much needed financial and psychological independence. Egerton then published *Pride and Prejudice*, a revision of *First Impressions*, in January 1813. He advertised the book widely and it was an immediate success, garnering three favourable reviews and selling well. *Mansfield Park* followed, but was not popular, and the failure of this title offset most of the profits Austen earned on Emma. These were the last of Austen's novels to be published during her lifetime. She wrote two additional novels, *Northanger Abbey* and *Persuasion*, both published posthumously in 1818, and began a third, which was eventually titled *Sanditon,* but died before completing it.

Early in 1816, Jane Austen began to feel unwell. She ignored her illness at first and continued to work and to participate in the usual round of family activities. By the middle of that year, her decline was unmistakable to Austen and to her family, and Austen's physical condition began a long, slow deterioration, culminating in her death the following year. Some biographers assign her symptoms to Addison's disease, and others to Hodgkin's lymphoma or even bovine tuberculosis from drinking unpasteurised milk; she was weak and couldn't walk from stiff joints. Austen died in Winchester, whilst seeking medical treatment, on 18th July 1817, at the age of forty-one. She is buried in the north aisle of the nave of Winchester Cathedral.

Austen's works critique the novels of sensibility of the second half of the eighteenth century and are part of the transition to nineteenth century realism. Her plots, though fundamentally comic, highlight the dependence of women on marriage to secure social standing and economic security. Her works though usually popular, were first published anonymously and brought her little personal fame and only a few positive reviews during her lifetime. It was the publication in 1869 of her nephew's *A Memoir of Jane Austen* that introduced her to a wider public, and by the 1940s she had become widely accepted in academia as a great English writer. The second half of the twentieth century saw a proliferation of Austen scholarship and the emergence of a Janeite fan culture. Her novels are still well-read, studied and loved right up to the present day.

A COLLECTION OF LETTERS

To Miss COOPER

COUSIN Conscious of the Charming Character which in
every Country, and every Clime in Christendom is Cried,
Concerning you, with Caution and Care I Commend
to your Charitable Criticism this Clever Collection of
Curious Comments, which have been Carefully Culled,
Collected and Classed by your Comical Cousin

The Author.

A COLLECTION OF LETTERS

LETTER the FIRST
From a MOTHER to her FREIND.

My Children begin now to claim all my attention in different Manner from that in which they have been used to receive it, as they are now arrived at that age when it is necessary for them in some measure to become conversant with the World, My Augusta is 17 and her sister scarcely a twelvemonth younger. I flatter myself that their education has been such as will not disgrace their appearance in the World, and that THEY will not disgrace their Education I have every reason to beleive. Indeed they are sweet Girls—. Sensible yet unaffected—Accomplished yet Easy—. Lively yet Gentle—. As their progress in every thing they have learnt has been always the same, I am willing to forget the difference of age, and to introduce them together into Public. This very Evening is fixed on as their first ENTREE into Life, as we are to drink tea with Mrs Cope and her Daughter. I am glad that we are to meet no one, for my Girls sake, as it would be awkward for them to enter too wide a Circle on the very first day. But we shall proceed by degrees.—Tomorrow Mr Stanly's family will drink tea with us, and perhaps the Miss Phillips's will meet them. On Tuesday we shall pay Morning Visits—On Wednesday we are to dine at Westbrook. On Thursday we have Company at home. On Friday we are to be at a Private Concert at Sir John

Wynna's—and on Saturday we expect Miss Dawson to call in the Morning—which will complete my Daughters Introduction into Life. How they will bear so much dissipation I cannot imagine; of their spirits I have no fear, I only dread their health.

This mighty affair is now happily over, and my Girls are OUT. As the moment approached for our departure, you can have no idea how the sweet Creatures trembled with fear and expectation. Before the Carriage drove to the door, I called them into my dressing-room, and as soon as they were seated thus addressed them. "My dear Girls the moment is now arrived when I am to reap the rewards of all my Anxieties and Labours towards you during your Education. You are this Evening to enter a World in which you will meet with many wonderfull Things; Yet let me warn you against suffering yourselves to be meanly swayed by the Follies and Vices of others, for beleive me my beloved Children that if you do—I shall be very sorry for it." They both assured me that they would ever remember my advice with Gratitude, and follow it with attention; That they were prepared to find a World full of things to amaze and to shock them: but that they trusted their behaviour would never give me reason to repent the Watchful Care with which I had presided over their infancy and formed their Minds—" "With such expectations and such intentions (cried I) I can have nothing to fear from you—and can chearfully conduct you to Mrs Cope's without a fear of your being seduced by her Example, or contaminated by her Follies. Come, then my Children (added I) the Carriage is driving to the door, and I will not a moment delay the happiness you are so impatient to enjoy." When we arrived at Warleigh, poor Augusta could scarcely breathe, while Margaret was all Life and Rapture. "The long-expected Moment is now arrived (said she) and we shall soon be in the World."—In a few Moments we were in Mrs Cope's parlour, where with her daughter she sate ready to receive us. I observed with delight the impression my Children made on them—. They were indeed two sweet, elegant-looking Girls, and tho' somewhat abashed from the peculiarity of their situation, yet there was an ease in their Manners and address which could not fail of pleasing—. Imagine my dear Madam how delighted I must have been in beholding as I did, how attentively they observed every object they saw, how disgusted with some Things, how enchanted with others, how astonished at all! On the whole however they returned in raptures with the World, its Inhabitants, and Manners. Yrs Ever—A. F.

LETTER the SECOND
From a YOUNG LADY
crossed in Love to her freind

———————————

Why should this last disappointment hang so heavily on my spirits? Why should I feel it more, why should it wound me deeper than those I have experienced before? Can it be that I have a greater affection for Willoughby than I had for his amiable predecessors? Or is it that our feelings become more acute from being often wounded? I must suppose my dear Belle that this is the Case, since I am not conscious of being more sincerely attached to Willoughby than I was to Neville, Fitzowen, or either of the Crawfords, for all of whom I once felt the most lasting affection that ever warmed a Woman's heart. Tell me then dear Belle why I still sigh when I think of the faithless Edward, or why I weep when I behold his Bride, for too surely this is the case—. My Freinds are all alarmed for me; They fear my declining health; they lament my want of spirits; they dread the effects of both. In hopes of releiving my melancholy, by directing my thoughts to other objects, they have invited several of their freinds to spend the Christmas with us. Lady Bridget Darkwood and her sister-in-law, Miss Jane are expected on Friday; and Colonel Seaton's family will be with us next week. This is all most kindly meant by my Uncle and Cousins; but what can the presence of a dozen indefferent people do to me, but weary and distress me—. I will not finish my Letter till some of our Visitors are arrived.

Friday Evening Lady Bridget came this morning, and with her, her sweet sister Miss Jane—. Although I have been acquainted with this charming Woman above fifteen Years, yet I never before observed how lovely she is. She is now about 35, and in spite of sickness, sorrow and Time is more blooming than I ever saw a Girl of 17. I was delighted with her, the moment she entered the house, and she appeared equally pleased with me, attaching herself to me during the remainder of the day. There is something so sweet, so mild in her Countenance, that she seems more than Mortal. Her Conversation is as bewitching as her appearance; I could not help telling her how much she engaged my admiration—. "Oh! Miss Jane (said I)—and stopped from an inability at the moment of expressing myself as I could wish—Oh! Miss Jane—(I repeated)—I could not think of words to suit my feelings—She seemed waiting for my speech—. I was confused—distressed—my thoughts were bewildered—and I could only add—"How do you do?" She saw and felt for my Embarrassment and with admirable presence of mind releived me from it by saying—"My dear Sophia be not uneasy at having exposed yourself—I will turn the Conversation without appearing to notice it. "Oh! how I loved her for her kindness!" Do you ride as much as you used to do?" said she—. "I am advised to ride by my Physician. We have delightful Rides round us, I have a Charming horse, am uncommonly fond of the Amusement, replied I quite recovered from my Confusion, and in short I ride a great deal." "You are in the right my Love," said she. Then repeating the following line which was an extempore and equally adapted to recommend both Riding and Candour—

"Ride where you may, Be Candid where you can," she added," I rode once, but it is many years ago—She spoke this in so low and tremulous a Voice, that I was silent—. Struck with her Manner

14

of speaking I could make no reply. "I have not ridden, continued she fixing her Eyes on my face, since I was married." I was never so surprised—"Married, Ma'am!" I repeated. "You may well wear that look of astonishment, said she, since what I have said must appear improbable to you—Yet nothing is more true than that I once was married."

"Then why are you called Miss Jane?"

"I married, my Sophia without the consent or knowledge of my father the late Admiral Annesley. It was therefore necessary to keep the secret from him and from every one, till some fortunate opportunity might offer of revealing it—. Such an opportunity alas! was but too soon given in the death of my dear Capt. Dashwood—Pardon these tears, continued Miss Jane wiping her Eyes, I owe them to my Husband's memory. He fell my Sophia, while fighting for his Country in America after a most happy Union of seven years—. My Children, two sweet Boys and a Girl, who had constantly resided with my Father and me, passing with him and with every one as the Children of a Brother (tho' I had ever been an only Child) had as yet been the comforts of my Life. But no sooner had I lossed my Henry, than these sweet Creatures fell sick and died—. Conceive dear Sophia what my feelings must have been when as an Aunt I attended my Children to their early Grave—. My Father did not survive them many weeks—He died, poor Good old man, happily ignorant to his last hour of my Marriage.'

"But did not you own it, and assume his name at your husband's death?"

"No; I could not bring myself to do it; more especially when in my Children I lost all inducement for doing it. Lady Bridget, and yourself are the only persons who are in the knowledge of my having ever been either Wife or Mother. As I could not Prevail on myself to take the name of Dashwood (a name which after my Henry's death I could never hear without emotion) and as I was conscious of having no right to that of Annesley, I dropt all thoughts of either, and have made it a point of bearing only my

Christian one since my Father's death." She paused—"Oh! my dear Miss Jane (said I) how infinitely am I obliged to you for so entertaining a story! You cannot think how it has diverted me! But have you quite done?"

"I have only to add my dear Sophia, that my Henry's elder Brother dieing about the same time, Lady Bridget became a Widow like myself, and as we had always loved each other in idea from the high Character in which we had ever been spoken of, though we had never met, we determined to live together. We wrote to one another on the same subject by the same post, so exactly did our feeling and our actions coincide! We both eagerly embraced the proposals we gave and received of becoming one family, and have from that time lived together in the greatest affection."

"And is this all? said I, I hope you have not done."

"Indeed I have; and did you ever hear a story more pathetic?"

"I never did—and it is for that reason it pleases me so much, for when one is unhappy nothing is so delightful to one's sensations as to hear of equal misery."

"Ah! but my Sophia why are YOU unhappy?"

"Have you not heard Madam of Willoughby's Marriage?"

"But my love why lament HIS perfidy, when you bore so well that of many young Men before?"

"Ah! Madam, I was used to it then, but when Willoughby broke his Engagements I had not been dissapointed for half a year."

"Poor Girl!" said Miss Jane.

LETTER the THIRD
From a YOUNG LADY
in distressed Circumstances to her

---

freind

A few days ago I was at a private Ball given by Mr Ashburnham. As my Mother never goes out she entrusted me to the care of Lady Greville who did me the honour of calling for me in her way and of allowing me to sit forwards, which is a favour about which I am very indifferent especially as I know it is considered as confering a great obligation on me "So Miss Maria (said her Ladyship as she saw me advancing to the door of the Carriage) you seem very smart to night—MY poor Girls will appear quite to disadvantage by YOU—I only hope your Mother may not have distressed herself to set YOU off. Have you got a new Gown on?"

"Yes Ma'am." replied I with as much indifference as I could assume.

"Aye, and a fine one too I think—(feeling it, as by her permission I seated myself by her) I dare say it is all very smart— But I must own, for you know I always speak my mind, that I think it was quite a needless piece of expence—Why could not you have worn your old striped one? It is not my way to find fault with People because they are poor, for I always think that they are more to be despised and pitied than blamed for it, especially if they cannot help it, but at the same time I must say that in my opinion your old striped Gown would have been quite fine enough for its Wearer—for to tell you the truth (I always speak my mind) I am very much afraid that one half of the people in the room will not know whether you have a Gown on or not— But I suppose you intend to make your fortune to night—. Well, the sooner the better; and I wish you success."

"Indeed Ma'am I have no such intention—"

"Who ever heard a young Lady own that she was a Fortune-hunter?" Miss Greville laughed but I am sure Ellen felt for me.

"Was your Mother gone to bed before you left her?" said her Ladyship.

"Dear Ma'am, said Ellen it is but nine o'clock."

"True Ellen, but Candles cost money, and Mrs Williams is too wise to be extravagant."

"She was just sitting down to supper Ma'am."

"And what had she got for supper?" "I did not observe." "Bread and Cheese I suppose." "I should never wish for a better supper." said Ellen. "You have never any reason replied her Mother, as a better is always provided for you." Miss Greville laughed excessively, as she constantly does at her Mother's wit.

Such is the humiliating Situation in which I am forced to appear while riding in her Ladyship's Coach—I dare not be impertinent, as my Mother is always admonishing me to be humble and patient if I wish to make my way in the world. She insists on my accepting every invitation of Lady Greville, or you may be certain that I would never enter either her House, or her Coach with the disagreable certainty I always have of being abused for my Poverty while I am in them.—When we arrived at Ashburnham, it was nearly ten o'clock, which was an hour and a half later than we were desired to be there; but Lady Greville is too fashionable (or fancies herself to be so) to be punctual. The Dancing however was not begun as they waited for Miss Greville. I had not been long in the room before I was engaged to dance by Mr Bernard, but just as we were going to stand up, he recollected that his Servant had got his white Gloves, and immediately ran out to fetch them. In the mean time the Dancing began and Lady Greville in passing to another room went exactly before me— She saw me and instantly stopping, said to me though there were several people close to us,

"Hey day, Miss Maria! What cannot you get a partner? Poor

Young Lady! I am afraid your new Gown was put on for nothing. But do not despair; perhaps you may get a hop before the Evening is over." So saying, she passed on without hearing my repeated assurance of being engaged, and leaving me very much provoked at being so exposed before every one—Mr Bernard however soon returned and by coming to me the moment he entered the room, and leading me to the Dancers my Character I hope was cleared from the imputation Lady Greville had thrown on it, in the eyes of all the old Ladies who had heard her speech. I soon forgot all my vexations in the pleasure of dancing and of having the most agreable partner in the room. As he is moreover heir to a very large Estate I could see that Lady Greville did not look very well pleased when she found who had been his Choice—She was determined to mortify me, and accordingly when we were sitting down between the dances, she came to me with more than her usual insulting importance attended by Miss Mason and said loud enough to be heard by half the people in the room, "Pray Miss Maria in what way of business was your Grandfather? for Miss Mason and I cannot agree whether he was a Grocer or a Bookbinder." I saw that she wanted to mortify me, and was resolved if I possibly could to Prevent her seeing that her scheme succeeded. "Neither Madam; he was a Wine Merchant." "Aye, I knew he was in some such low way—He broke did not he?" "I beleive not Ma'am." "Did not he abscond?" "I never heard that he did." "At least he died insolvent?" "I was never told so before." "Why, was not your FATHER as poor as a Rat" "I fancy not." "Was not he in the Kings Bench once?" "I never saw him there." She gave me SUCH a look, and turned away in a great passion; while I was half delighted with myself for my impertinence, and half afraid of being thought too saucy. As Lady Greville was extremely angry with me, she took no further notice of me all the Evening, and indeed had I been in favour I should have been equally neglected, as she was got into a Party of great folks and she never speaks to me when she can to anyone else. Miss Greville was with her Mother's party at supper, but Ellen preferred staying with the Bernards and me. We had a very pleasant Dance and as Lady G—slept all the way home, I had a very comfortable ride.

The next day while we were at dinner Lady Greville's Coach stopped at the door, for that is the time of day she generally contrives it should. She sent in a message by the servant to say that "she should not get out but that Miss Maria must come to the Coach-door, as she wanted to speak to her, and that she must make haste and come immediately—" "What an impertinent Message Mama!" said I—"Go Maria—" replied she—Accordingly I went and was obliged to stand there at her Ladyships pleasure though the Wind was extremely high and very cold.

"Why I think Miss Maria you are not quite so smart as you were last night—But I did not come to examine your dress, but to tell you that you may dine with us the day after tomorrow— Not tomorrow, remember, do not come tomorrow, for we expect Lord and Lady Clermont and Sir Thomas Stanley's family— There will be no occasion for your being very fine for I shant send the Carriage—If it rains you may take an umbrella—" I could hardly help laughing at hearing her give me leave to keep myself dry—"And pray remember to be in time, for I shant wait—I hate my Victuals over-done—But you need not come before the time—How does your Mother do? She is at dinner is not she?" "Yes Ma'am we were in the middle of dinner when your Ladyship came." "I am afraid you find it very cold Maria." said Ellen. "Yes, it is an horrible East wind—said her Mother—I assure you I can hardly bear the window down—But you are used to be blown about by the wind Miss Maria and that is what has made your Complexion so rudely and coarse. You young Ladies who cannot often ride in a Carriage never mind what weather you trudge in, or how the wind shews your legs. I would not have my Girls stand out of doors as you do in such a day as this. But some sort of people have no feelings either of cold or Delicacy—Well, remember that we shall expect you on Thursday at 5 o'clock— You must tell your Maid to come for you at night—There will be no Moon—and you will have an horrid walk home—My compts to Your Mother—I am afraid your dinner will be cold—Drive on—" And away she went, leaving me in a great passion with her as she always does. Maria Williams.

LETTER the FOURTH
From a YOUNG LADY
rather impertinent to her freind

We dined yesterday with Mr Evelyn where we were introduced to a very agreable looking Girl his Cousin. I was extremely pleased with her appearance, for added to the charms of an engaging face, her manner and voice had something peculiarly interesting in them. So much so, that they inspired me with a great curiosity to know the history of her Life, who were her Parents, where she came from, and what had befallen her, for it was then only known that she was a relation of Mr Evelyn, and that her name was Grenville. In the evening a favourable opportunity offered to me of attempting at least to know what I wished to know, for every one played at Cards but Mrs Evelyn, My Mother, Dr Drayton, Miss Grenville and myself, and as the two former were engaged in a whispering Conversation, and the Doctor fell asleep, we were of necessity obliged to entertain each other. This was what I wished and being determined not to remain in ignorance for want of asking, I began the Conversation in the following Manner.

"Have you been long in Essex Ma'am?"

"I arrived on Tuesday."

"You came from Derbyshire?"

"No, Ma'am! appearing surprised at my question, from Suffolk." You will think this a good dash of mine my dear Mary, but you know that I am not wanting for Impudence when I have any end in veiw. "Are you pleased with the Country Miss Grenville? Do you find it equal to the one you have left?"

"Much superior Ma'am in point of Beauty." She sighed. I longed to know for why.

"But the face of any Country however beautiful said I, can be but a poor consolation for the loss of one's dearest Freinds." She shook her head, as if she felt the truth of what I said. My Curiosity was so much raised, that I was resolved at any rate to satisfy it.

"You regret having left Suffolk then Miss Grenville?" "Indeed I do." "You were born there I suppose?" "Yes Ma'am I was and passed many happy years there—"

"That is a great comfort—said I—I hope Ma'am that you never spent any unhappy one's there."

"Perfect Felicity is not the property of Mortals, and no one has a right to expect uninterrupted Happiness.—Some Misfortunes I have certainly met with."

"WHAT Misfortunes dear Ma'am? replied I, burning with impatience to know every thing. "NONE Ma'am I hope that have been the effect of any wilfull fault in me." "I dare say not Ma'am, and have no doubt but that any sufferings you may have experienced could arise only from the cruelties of Relations or the Errors of Freinds." She sighed—"You seem unhappy my dear Miss Grenville—Is it in my power to soften your Misfortunes?" "YOUR power Ma'am replied she extremely surprised; it is in NO ONES power to make me happy." She pronounced these words in so mournfull and solemn an accent, that for some time I had not courage to reply. I was actually silenced. I recovered myself however in a few moments and looking at her with all the affection I could, "My dear Miss Grenville said I, you appear extremely young—and may probably stand in need of some one's advice whose regard for you, joined to superior Age, perhaps superior Judgement might authorise her to give it. I am that person, and I now challenge you to accept the offer I make you of my Confidence and Freindship, in return to which I shall only ask for yours—"

"You are extremely obliging Ma'am—said she—and I am highly flattered by your attention to me—But I am in no difficulty, no doubt, no uncertainty of situation in which any advice can be wanted. Whenever I am however continued she brightening into a complaisant smile, I shall know where to apply."

I bowed, but felt a good deal mortified by such a repulse; still however I had not given up my point. I found that by the appearance of sentiment and Freindship nothing was to be gained and determined therefore to renew my attacks by Questions and suppositions. "Do you intend staying long in this part of England Miss Grenville?"

"Yes Ma'am, some time I beleive."

"But how will Mr and Mrs Grenville bear your absence?"

"They are neither of them alive Ma'am." This was an answer I did not expect—I was quite silenced, and never felt so awkward in my Life—-.

LETTER the FIFTH
From a YOUNG LADY
very much in love to her Freind

My Uncle gets more stingy, my Aunt more particular, and I more in love every day. What shall we all be at this rate by the end of the year! I had this morning the happiness of receiving the following Letter from my dear Musgrove.

Sackville St: Janry 7th It is a month to day since I first beheld my lovely Henrietta, and the sacred anniversary must and shall be kept in a manner becoming the day—by writing to her. Never shall I forget the moment when her Beauties first broke on my sight—No time as you well know can erase it from my Memory. It was at Lady Scudamores. Happy Lady Scudamore to live within a mile of the divine Henrietta! When the lovely Creature first entered the room, oh! what were my sensations? The sight of you was like the sight of a wonderful fine Thing. I started—I gazed at her with admiration—She appeared every moment more Charming, and the unfortunate Musgrove became a captive to your Charms before I had time to look about me. Yes Madam, I had the happiness of adoring you, an happiness for which I cannot be too grateful. "What said he to himself is Musgrove allowed to die for Henrietta? Enviable Mortal! and may he pine for her who is the object of universal admiration, who is adored by a Colonel, and toasted by a Baronet! Adorable Henrietta how beautiful you are! I declare you are quite divine! You are more than Mortal. You are an Angel. You are Venus herself. In short Madam you are the prettiest Girl I ever saw in my Life—and her Beauty is encreased in her Musgroves Eyes, by permitting him to love her and allowing me to hope. And ah! Angelic Miss Henrietta Heaven is my witness how ardently I do hope for the death of your villanous Uncle and his abandoned Wife, since my fair one will not consent to be mine till their decease has placed her in affluence above what my fortune can procure—. Though it is an improvable Estate—. Cruel Henrietta to persist in such a resolution! I am at Present with my sister where I mean to continue till my own house which tho' an excellent one is at Present somewhat out of repair, is ready to receive me. Amiable princess of my Heart farewell—Of that Heart which trembles while it signs itself Your most ardent Admirer and devoted humble servt. T. Musgrove.

There is a pattern for a Love-letter Matilda! Did you ever read such a master-piece of Writing? Such sense, such sentiment, such purity of Thought, such flow of Language and such unfeigned Love in one sheet? No, never I can answer for it, since a Musgrove is not to be met with by every Girl. Oh! how I long to be with him! I intend to send him the following in answer to his Letter tomorrow.

My dearest Musgrove—. Words cannot express how happy your Letter made me; I thought I should have cried for joy, for I love you better than any body in the World. I think you the most amiable, and the handsomest Man in England, and so to be sure you are. I never read so sweet a Letter in my Life. Do write me another just like it, and tell me you are in love with me in every other line. I quite die to see you. How shall we manage to see one another? for we are so much in love that we cannot live asunder. Oh! my dear Musgrove you cannot think how impatiently I wait for the death of my Uncle and Aunt—If they will not Die soon, I beleive I shall run mad, for I get more in love with you every day of my Life.

How happy your Sister is to enjoy the pleasure of your Company in her house, and how happy every body in London must be because you are there. I hope you will be so kind as to write to me again soon, for I never read such sweet Letters as yours. I am my dearest Musgrove most truly and faithfully yours for ever and ever Henrietta Halton.

I hope he will like my answer; it is as good a one as I can write though nothing to his; Indeed I had always heard what a dab he was at a Love-letter. I saw him you know for the first time at Lady Scudamores—And when I saw her Ladyship afterwards she asked me how I liked her Cousin Musgrove?

"Why upon my word said I, I think he is a very handsome young Man."

"I am glad you think so replied she, for he is distractedly in love with you."

"Law! Lady Scudamore said I, how can you talk so ridiculously?"

"Nay, t'is very true answered she, I assure you, for he was in love with you from the first moment he beheld you."

"I wish it may be true said I, for that is the only kind of love I would give a farthing for—There is some sense in being in love at first sight."

"Well, I give you Joy of your conquest, replied Lady Scudamore, and I beleive it to have been a very complete one; I am sure it is not a contemptible one, for my Cousin is a charming young fellow, has seen a great deal of the World, and writes the best Love-letters I ever read."

This made me very happy, and I was excessively pleased with my conquest. However, I thought it was proper to give myself a few Airs—so I said to her—

"This is all very pretty Lady Scudamore, but you know that we young Ladies who are Heiresses must not throw ourselves away upon Men who have no fortune at all."

"My dear Miss Halton said she, I am as much convinced of that as you can be, and I do assure you that I should be the last person to encourage your marrying anyone who had not some pretensions to expect a fortune with you. Mr Musgrove is so far from being poor that he has an estate of several hundreds an year which is capable of great Improvement, and an excellent House, though at Present it is not quite in repair."

"If that is the case replied I, I have nothing more to say against him, and if as you say he is an informed young Man and can write a good Love-letter, I am sure I have no reason to find fault with him for admiring me, tho' perhaps I may not marry him for all that Lady Scudamore."

"You are certainly under no obligation to marry him answered her Ladyship, except that which love himself will dictate to you, for if I am not greatly mistaken you are at this very moment unknown to yourself, cherishing a most tender affection for him."

"Law, Lady Scudamore replied I blushing how can you think of such a thing?"

"Because every look, every word betrays it, answered she; Come my dear Henrietta, consider me as a freind, and be sincere with me—Do not you prefer Mr Musgrove to any man of your acquaintance?"

"Pray do not ask me such questions Lady Scudamore, said I turning away my head, for it is not fit for me to answer them."

"Nay my Love replied she, now you confirm my suspicions. But why Henrietta should you be ashamed to own a well-placed Love, or why refuse to confide in me?"

"I am not ashamed to own it; said I taking Courage. I do not refuse to confide in you or blush to say that I do love your cousin Mr Musgrove, that I am sincerely attached to him, for it is no disgrace to love a handsome Man. If he were plain indeed I might have had reason to be ashamed of a passion which must have been mean since the object would have been unworthy. But with such a figure and face, and such beautiful hair as your Cousin has, why should I blush to own that such superior merit has made an impression on me."

"My sweet Girl (said Lady Scudamore embracing me with great affection) what a delicate way of thinking you have in these matters, and what a quick discernment for one of your years! Oh! how I honour you for such Noble Sentiments!"

"Do you Ma'am said I; You are vastly obliging. But pray Lady Scudamore did your Cousin himself tell you of his affection for me I shall like him the better if he did, for what is a Lover without a Confidante?"

"Oh! my Love replied she, you were born for each other. Every word you say more deeply convinces me that your Minds are actuated by the invisible power of simpathy, for your opinions and sentiments so exactly coincide. Nay, the colour of your Hair is not very different. Yes my dear Girl, the poor despairing Musgrove did reveal to me the story of his Love—. Nor was I surprised at it—I know not how it was, but I had a kind of presentiment that he would be in love with you."

"Well, but how did he break it to you?"

"It was not till after supper. We were sitting round the fire together talking on indifferent subjects, though to say the truth the Conversation was cheifly on my side for he was thoughtful and silent, when on a sudden he interrupted me in the midst of something I was saying, by exclaiming in a most Theatrical tone—

Yes I'm in love I feel it now And Henrietta Halton has undone me

"Oh! What a sweet way replied I, of declaring his Passion! To make such a couple of charming lines about me! What a pity it is that they are not in rhime!"

"I am very glad you like it answered she; To be sure there was a great deal of Taste in it. And are you in love with her, Cousin? said I. I am very sorry for it, for unexceptionable as you are in every respect, with a pretty Estate capable of Great improvements, and an excellent House tho' somewhat out of repair, yet who can hope to aspire with success to the adorable Henrietta who has had an offer from a Colonel and been toasted by a Baronet"— "THAT I have—" cried I. Lady Scudamore continued. "Ah dear Cousin replied he, I am so well convinced of the little Chance I can have of winning her who is adored by thousands, that I need no assurances of yours to make me more thoroughly so. Yet surely neither you or the fair Henrietta herself will deny me the exquisite Gratification of dieing for her, of falling a victim to her Charms. And when I am dead"—continued her—

"Oh Lady Scudamore, said I wiping my eyes, that such a sweet Creature should talk of dieing!"

"It is an affecting Circumstance indeed, replied Lady Scudamore." "When I am dead said he, let me be carried and lain at her feet, and perhaps she may not disdain to drop a pitying tear on my poor remains."

"Dear Lady Scudamore interrupted I, say no more on this affecting subject. I cannot bear it."

"Oh! how I admire the sweet sensibility of your Soul, and as I would not for Worlds wound it too deeply, I will be silent."

"Pray go on." said I. She did so.

"And then added he, Ah! Cousin imagine what my transports will be when I feel the dear precious drops trickle on my face! Who would not die to haste such extacy! And when I am interred, may the divine Henrietta bless some happier Youth with her affection, May he be as tenderly attached to her as the hapless Musgrove and while HE crumbles to dust, May they live an example of Felicity in the Conjugal state!"

Did you ever hear any thing so pathetic? What a charming wish, to be lain at my feet when he was dead! Oh! what an exalted mind he must have to be capable of such a wish! Lady Scudamore went on.

"Ah! my dear Cousin replied I to him, such noble behaviour as this, must melt the heart of any woman however obdurate it may naturally be; and could the divine Henrietta but hear your generous wishes for her happiness, all gentle as is her mind, I have not a doubt but that she would pity your affection and endeavour to return it." "Oh! Cousin answered he, do not endeavour to raise my hopes by such flattering assurances. No, I cannot hope to please this angel of a Woman, and the only thing which remains for me to do, is to die." "True Love is ever desponding replied I, but I my dear Tom will give you even greater hopes of conquering this fair one's heart, than I have yet given you, by assuring you that I watched her with the strictest attention during the whole day, and could plainly discover that she cherishes in her bosom though unknown to herself, a most tender affection for you."

"Dear Lady Scudamore cried I, This is more than I ever knew!"

"Did not I say that it was unknown to yourself? I did not, continued I to him, encourage you by saying this at first, that surprise might render the pleasure still Greater." "No Cousin replied he in a languid voice, nothing will convince me that I can have touched the heart of Henrietta Halton, and if you are deceived yourself, do not attempt deceiving me." "In short my Love it was the work of some hours for me to Persuade the poor despairing Youth that you had really a preference for him; but when at last he could no longer deny the force of my arguments, or discredit what I told him, his transports, his Raptures, his Extacies are beyond my power to describe."

"Oh! the dear Creature, cried I, how passionately he loves me! But dear Lady Scudamore did you tell him that I was totally dependant on my Uncle and Aunt?"

"Yes, I told him every thing."

"And what did he say."

"He exclaimed with virulence against Uncles and Aunts; Accused the laws of England for allowing them to Possess their Estates when wanted by their Nephews or Neices, and wished HE were in the House of Commons, that he might reform the Legislature, and rectify all its abuses."

"Oh! the sweet Man! What a spirit he has!" said I.

"He could not flatter himself he added, that the adorable Henrietta would condescend for his sake to resign those Luxuries and that splendor to which she had been used, and accept only in exchange the Comforts and Elegancies which his limited Income could afford her, even supposing that his house were in Readiness to receive her. I told him that it could not be expected that she would; it would be doing her an injustice to suppose her capable of giving up the power she now possesses and so nobly uses of doing such extensive Good to the poorer part of her fellow Creatures, merely for the gratification of you and herself."

"To be sure said I, I AM very Charitable every now and then. And what did Mr Musgrove say to this?"

"He replied that he was under a melancholy necessity of owning the truth of what I said, and that therefore if he should be the happy Creature destined to be the Husband of the Beautiful Henrietta he must bring himself to wait, however impatiently, for the fortunate day, when she might be freed from the power of worthless Relations and able to bestow herself on him."

What a noble Creature he is! Oh! Matilda what a fortunate one I am, who am to be his Wife! My Aunt is calling me to come and make the pies, so adeiu my dear freind, and beleive me yours etc—H. Halton.

Finis.

SCRAPS

To Miss FANNY CATHERINE AUSTEN

MY Dear Neice As I am prevented by the great distance between Rowling and Steventon from superintending your Education myself, the care of which will probably on that account devolve on your Father and Mother, I think it is my particular Duty to Prevent your feeling as much as possible the want of my personal instructions, by addressing to you on paper my Opinions and Admonitions on the conduct of Young Women, which you will find expressed in the following pages.—I am my dear Neice Your affectionate Aunt The Author.

Lightning Source UK Ltd.
Milton Keynes UK
UKHW011437021120
372651UK00003B/671